It's Cold Outside! Where Is Your Jacket?

By Diane Orr, the Farmer

A 'de Good Life Farm' Story
Book 6

It's Cold Outside. Where Is Your Jacket? by Diane Orr

Published by Pen It! Publications, LLC 812-371-4128 www.penitpublications.com

Published in the United States of America by Pen It! Publications, LLC

ISBN: 978-1-63984-003-8

Photographs provided by the Author

DEDICATION

This book is dedicated to my granddaughter, Emma, who by asking me a simple question, inspired this book. It is also dedicated to my other grandchildren: James, Annalise, Emery, Harper, Hunter and Garrett, who enjoy spending time at de Good Life Farm.

SPECIAL THANKS TO

To my friends for allowing me to take pictures of their animals that we do not have here on de Good Life Farm:

Jamie Padovano and her farm,

"Garrett's Goaty Acres",

For pictures of her goats, ducks and horses,

And

Jodi and Katie Oberdier and their farm,

"The Jordan River Farm",

For pictures of their sheep,

And to,

Brandy Orndorf

Of

"The Spotted Pig Ranch"

For allowing me to use her picture of Pearl, the pig.

There is Merlin, the rooster and his hens.
"Hey Merlin, it's cold outside! Where is your jacket?"

"We don't need jackets!

Our Creator gave us feathers that we can fluff up!
When we fluff up our feathers, it creates tiny air pockets between them.
These tiny air pockets are warmed by our body heat so we can stay warm."

There is Mocha being silly in the pasture with Jersey.
"Hey, cows! It's cold outside!
Where are your jackets?"

"We don't need jackets.

Our Creator gave us thick skin, coarse hair and healthy fat as a natural insulator from the cold. Our Creator also gave us a rumen that allows the grass and hay we eat to be turned into energy which acts like a furnace and keeps us warm. We actually prefer cold weather!"

There is Odin, the livestock guardian dog!

"Hey, Odin! It's cold outside! Where is your jacket?"

"I don't need a jacket!

My Creator gave me a weather-resistant double coat that consists of a thick, coarse overcoat and a warm wooly undercoat. I can stand out in the rain, snow or ice and the weather will never touch my skin because of my special coats of fur."

There is Pearl, the pig.

"Hey, Pearl, it's cold outside. Where is your jacket?"

"I don't need a jacket.

My Creator gave me a big appetite and thick skin. The more I eat in the winter, the more my body can produce natural body heat. So, I like to eat a lot in the winter!"

There are the barn cats, Ollie and Gandalf!

"Hey, kitty, kitty! It's cold outside!
Where are your jackets?"

"We don't need jackets!

Our Creator made our fur grow thick in the winter. We also like to curl up and tuck in our paws and noses, which keeps our body heat from escaping."

There is Ida, the sheep, with her lambs!

"Hey, Ida! It's cold outside!

Where is your jacket?"

"I don't need a jacket!

My Creator gave me a wool coat that keeps my body heat in and the cold air out! Also, the lanolin in my wool keeps the moisture from getting to my skin!"

Look, there is the duck family!
"Hey, ducks, it's cold outside!
Where are your jackets?"

"We don't need jackets to keep us warm!

Our Creator gave us a preen gland that releases an oily substance all over our bodies when we clean our feathers using our beaks.
This oil acts as an insulator that keeps us warm and waterproof."

Smoke, Sundance, and Trinity, the horses, and Dominic, the miniature donkey are in the pasture! "Hey, everyone! It's cold outside! Where are your jackets?"

"We don't need jackets to keep us warm!

Our Creator gave us warm winter coats to protect us from the cold weather. Also, our bodies have the ability to generate heat when we eat grass or hay. Eating warms our bodies just as if we were running around and exercising."

There is Mr. Rabbit. "Hey, Mr. Rabbit!
It's cold outside!
Where is your jacket?"

"I don't need a jacket!

My Creator gave me more density in my winter coat than there is in my summer coat. If my coat turns to white, my white hair traps more air which means more insulation to keep me warm."

There is Snow, the goat.

"Hey, Snow, where is your jacket?"

"I don't need a jacket!

My Creator gave me a winter coat to keep me warm. Also, when I eat hay, it makes my rumen work which acts like a natural furnace to keep me warm from the inside out."

Hey, look! It's You!

It's cold outside! Where is your jacket?

"I have my jacket on!

My Creator made me different than all the animals and I need my jacket to stay warm in cold weather!"

There are many other animals on the farm.

None of them wear jackets!!

GLOSSARY

Coarse – not fine, delicate or soft

Density – the state of being dense or compact

Furnace - heater

Generate – to produce

Insulation, insulator – something that prevents heat from escaping

Lanolin – a wax substance secreted from the gland of a wool-bearing animal

Moisture – the presence of water in a very small amount

Oily – greasy

Preen gland – an oil gland located near the tail on many birds

Rumen – the first stomach of grazing animals

Waterproof – keeps water from soaking in

Weather-resistant – resists the effects of severe cold or rainy weather

Watch for other books in the ‘de Good Life Farm’
Story Series

My Name is Mocha
My Name is Merlin
We are Mocha’s Family
My Name is Odin
The Mysterious Midnight Visitor at de Good Life Farm

Watch for other de Good Life Farm books coming soon!

Author Diane Orr is so thankful to God to be a wife, mom and nana. She had the privilege of homeschooling her sons from kindergarten through their high school graduation. She loves books and has been writing stories and poems for most of her life.

She loves living on "de Good Life Farm" with her husband, Jeff, and her youngest son, Micah, and loves sharing the farm with her grandchildren and anyone who enjoys it. She is crazy about her cows and the other animals and enjoys taking care of them. They provide both entertainment and the inspiration from which many of her stories originate. Additionally, Diane also loves taking photographs of life on the farm so that other people may enjoy it vicariously.

Lightning Source UK Ltd.
Milton Keynes UK
UKHW052256290621
386380UK00002B/9